HENRY REED, INC.

from the tool shed. The shed was at least fifty feet from the house but that howl sounded as though the dog were standing right beneath the window. Aunt Mabel looked uncomfortable and Uncle Al didn't say a word. He just sat on the blanket chest and continued smoking. There was a short pause and then there was a second howl. Still no one said anything about it. With the third howl that beagle really hit his stride. The glass in the window beside the bed began to vibrate.

"He's not very happy," I said.

"So it would seem," Uncle Al replied.

"Do you think if we opened the door of the shed so he could wander around the yard it would help?" Aunt Mabel asked.

"No," Uncle Al replied, "but I'm willing to try."

"I'll go down and open the door," I volunteered.

"There's a flashlight on the kitchen table," said Uncle Al.

I went down and out the back door and opened the door to the shed. The beagle came trotting out. He didn't jump up on me or make any fuss. He just wagged his tail and trotted along at my heels as I went back toward the kitchen door. He looked up at me when I reached the door, as if asking for permission to go in. He is certainly a smart little dog.

"No," I said. "You stay out here."

I went back upstairs and was just inside the door of

my room when he started howling again. This time, since he was practically underneath my window, the noise was even louder than before. The whole room seemed to shake with it.

"What on earth is the matter with that dog?" my Aunt Mabel asked in an annoyed voice.

"I think maybe he's decided he likes Hank's room," Uncle Al said. That was sort of a silly statement, because of course the dog had never been up in my room.

"I don't like the idea of a stray dog in the house," said Aunt Mabel. "He might have fleas. At least he should have a bath."

"It's kind of late to give him one tonight," Uncle Al said. "It looks like the choice is between fleas or noise. We don't know that he has fleas and we do know that he howls."

"Maybe he's hungry," Aunt Mabel said. "I'll go down and see if I can find him something to eat."

I don't know much about beagles but I do know something about howls, and that wasn't a hungry howl. But I didn't say anything. Aunt Mabel and Uncle Al went downstairs to the kitchen while I changed into my pajamas. As I was getting undressed I noticed a book on the shelf about dogs so I got it down and looked up beagles.

The book didn't tell me much except that beagles were a very old breed and nobody knew exactly where they originated. The author thought that there was some fox-hound in them and possibly some bloodhound. Anyhow, they are supposed to be very companionable dogs, and to be very intelligent, and to have a sharp sense of smell. The book didn't say a thing about their howling at night, but it did say they had a wonderful musical bay when they were following a rabbit. I put on my bathrobe and went downstairs to the kitchen. The beagle was finishing some food that Aunt Mabel had given him. He looked up at me and wagged his tail.

"That's a smart dog," Uncle Al said. "He's got you spotted."

"Well, now that he's had something to eat let's try him again," Aunt Mabel said. She held open the kitchen screen and said, "Come on, outside, doggie. Outside you go."

The beagle went outside as politely as could be. I looked through the screen and saw him lie down at the foot of the steps. We turned out the light and left the kitchen for the living room.

"Shall we wait down here in the living room or shall we come back down again?" Uncle Al asked.

Aunt Mabel looked at the clock. "We might as well listen to the news."

Uncle Al turned on the television and found a news program. We had listened for about four or five minutes when the beagle began to howl again.

"How does it happen you know so much about research?"

"My father's a research chemist." She finished her apple and threw the core over into the grass.

I was still up on the ladder. I drew the lines a little bit longer and started roughing out the letters to make the words PURE AND APPLIED RESEARCH. I worked for several minutes and Midge didn't say a word.

"I might join your firm," she said finally, "if you invited me nicely."

"Why should I?"

"Teamwork," she answered. "Teamwork's the thing these days in research. My father says things have gotten so complicated that one man alone can't discover much any more."

I thought this over for a minute while I kept working on my sign. If her father was a research chemist like she said, she probably knew quite a bit about how research organizations work, and also with the whole summer ahead of me I figured it might be nice to have someone to talk to, even if it was a girl a year and a half younger than I. I turned around and sat down on the ladder.

"What are you going to put into the business?" I asked. "I've got the property here, the building, a lot of pigeons which are inside, and one turtle." I waved my hand up at the half-finished sign, which was pretty good. "I'm even furnishing the sign."

"I'll furnish brains," she said.

Even though I always try to be polite, I laughed out loud at that, but she didn't seem to mind.

"Brains are the most important part of any research organization. My father says so."

"He's probably right," I admitted. "But the question is who has them? What grade are you in?"

"Seventh," she replied.

"There you are," I said. "I'm in the eighth grade so I've had more education. I've had more experience, too. I'm a teen-ager and you're only twelve."

"That's no advantage," she said. "Who are all these delinquent children you read about in the papers? Teen-agers—that's you. Me, I'm not a teen-ager so I must be a respectable, law-abiding citizen."

She started laughing like an idiot again. I don't know what about, since her remark didn't even make any sense. I climbed down the ladder and put my can of paint and brush on a box. I sharpened my pencil and started toward the ladder again.

"I could also contribute a pair of rabbits," she said. "We could raise rabbits, and they use a lot of rabbits in research to test serum and drugs and feeds and things like that."

I thought this over for a minute. I've never had any rabbits because we have never lived anyplace where there was room enough. "What kind of rabbits?" I asked.

"Checkered Giants," Midge replied. "They're great big white rabbits with black spots."

"That might not be a bad idea," I said, "to have a few rabbits."

"You could just make that 'Reed and Glass, Inc.,'" she said, pointing up at my sign.

I had just finished painting the words "Henry Reed" and I didn't care much for the idea of changing my sign before it was half finished. "Let's see the rabbits first," I suggested.

She led the way across the street to a big white frame house which sat well back from the road. We went around the house to the back, past a little sunken stone-walled garden, and through a hedge to a small barn that was used for a garage. Beside this sat a little portable wire pen. Attached to one end of the pen was a tiny wooden house with a tarpaper roof. Only one rabbit was in sight. It was out in the pen, nibbling away at part of a carrot.

"That's Mathilda," Midge said.

Mathilda was an enormous rabbit. There was a small wire gate on top of the pen. I opened this, reached in, and picked her up. She weighed at least seven or eight pounds and was as strong and wiry as a wildcat. The minute I lifted her off the ground she started kicking like a mule and about the third or fourth kick she made several deep scratches in my wrist. I let her drop back down in the pen. She seemed healthy, all right.

Friday, June 28th

Business has been sort of slow all week. In fact, nothing happened since Mr. Apple's visit last Tuesday until today. Today I got a new product. I'm in the earthworm business now. So far it's been very profitable and quite interesting.

The way it happened was that the garden needed cultivating. There were quite a few weeds in between the rows and I suggested to Aunt Mabel that maybe I ought to get out the tractor and plow it. She agreed that the garden needed cultivating but said that Uncle Al would probably feel cheated when he got home.

"You go ahead, anyhow," she said. "Al will just have to share his tractor this summer, now that he's showed you how to use it."

I got the tractor out, figured out how to attach the cultivator on the back, and plowed the whole garden twice in less than an hour. The tractor works like a dream. Just as I was finishing, a man in a dark blue car stopped at the side of the road and walked over to the fence. "Are you turning up any worms?" he asked.

"Quite a few," I told him.

"How about selling me a couple of dozen?"

I looked at him closely and he looked perfectly normal. "You want to buy some worms?" I asked.

"Sure, haven't you ever heard of selling worms?"

"I've heard of selling snails and grasshoppers and rattlesnakes, but never worms," I said. "How do you cook them?"

"You don't cook them at all," he replied. "I'm going fishing. Look, I'd sooner pay you twenty-five cents a dozen, say, than dig them myself. First place, I live in an apartment and haven't any place to dig. Secondly, it's just too much bother. You might dig half an hour before you find the right spot. Sometimes you can't find any at all."

The garden was full of worms so I found a can, filled it with dirt, and picked up about two dozen large worms. He gave me fifty cents and drove off perfectly happy. I decided immediately to go into the earthworm business. I had already made the change in my sign that Uncle Al had suggested, except that I had listed just turtles and pigeons. There was no point in saying that I had rabbits to sell until I had more than one. Midge and I tried three different times during the week to catch that rabbit and each time he got away.

I went to the basement to get the can of white paint and a brush so that I could add earthworms to my sign.

On my way out of the house Aunt Mabel called to me from the kitchen.

"If you enjoy operating that little tractor, why don't you take the sickle bar and mow your lot?" she asked. "Al usually does it once or twice a year to keep the place from going completely to jungle."

I unhooked the cultivator and hooked the two-wheel cart on behind the tractor, put the sickle bar, paint, and brush in the cart, and drove off toward the lot. Agony as usual tagged along.

Midge appeared about ten seconds after I did, and immediately wanted to operate the tractor. She helped me hook up the sickle bar and I made a couple of turns around the lot, and cut a swath about three feet wide. Agony kept running ahead of the tractor so we had to tie him up. I was afraid I would cut off his legs.

I mowed for about half an hour and then turned the tractor over to Midge while I added EARTHWORMS to our sign. She finished mowing about the same time I finished painting. What with the whole end of the barn just about covered with the sign, and all the grass freshly cut, we looked pretty snappy.

"What are you going to keep the earthworms in?" she asked.

"Dirt," I replied.

"Yes, but you can't waste time going out and digging them every time someone wants to buy a few. Besides,

Thursday, July 4th

It is rather late but I think I will put down the day's events before I go to bed. This entry hasn't anything to do with private enterprise. It's simply about Independence Day. Since some of my class in Naples haven't been back in the United States for several years, I want to tell them about the Fourth of July and how it's celebrated. They may have a lot of wrong ideas just as I had.

All my life I've listened to my mother and father tell about how they celebrated the Fourth. They shot off firecrackers, threw torpedoes, shot roman candles, set off pinwheels and skyrockets, and stepped on red devils that cracked and popped. They made a racket all day long, burned their fingers, ate until they were sick, and had a wonderful, noisy time. No more. There aren't any fireworks. They're against the law in most states and New Jersey is one of them. Now you go sit in a big football stadium and watch someone else set off pinwheels and skyrockets. All the kids do now is fidget around on the hard cement seats and wait for the "boom."

Of course having the fireworks shot off for you is better than not having any at all. Uncle Al says that outlawing fireworks was a good thing because every year a number of people, usually children, got badly burned. Some were maimed for life and some were killed.

"Of course, now that we've made the glorious Fourth safe by banning fireworks," he said, "people take to the highways in droves and kill each other with their automobiles. I suppose I should take you down to the shore today but frankly I'm afraid to. I wouldn't drive anywhere for all the tea in China."

Aunt Mabel suggested that we go in for the fireworks at Palmer Stadium later and Uncle Al agreed. Since we can get to Princeton by the back roads, he was willing to drive that far.

Naturally I was disappointed about not having the kind of a Fourth my parents had told me about, but there was no use feeling sad about it. I decided to spend the day as I would a quiet Sunday, so I got a book and started to read. I was on the couch on the front porch and Uncle Al was puttering around some bushes beside the porch when a blue and white sedan exactly like Uncle Al's drove into the lane. Uncle Al looked around in annoyance and muttered something about visitors.

"It's Mr. Apple," I said in a low voice. "And he has a car exactly like yours."

"I know he has," Uncle Al said. "It doesn't make me like my car any better. However, I think he got his first so I shouldn't kick."

Mr. Apple got out of his car and marched across the

lawn like a small boy on his way to speak a piece in Sunday School. "Mr. Harris, I'm sorry but I have a complaint to make," he said. He didn't look a bit sorry.

"Yes, what's that?"

"That hound of your nephew's insists on coming over on my property and causing damage."

"What kind of damage?" Uncle Al asked, straightening up with a grunt.

"Well, he digs," Mr. Apple said. "Right in the center of my lawn."

Uncle Al looked at me with a question in his eyes. I nodded. "I saw him digging there once," I admitted. "I didn't know he had any other times."

"He is constantly running across my property," Mr. Apple said. "My wife has a cat and he frightens that. I don't think it's a bit too much to ask that he be kept on a leash."

"Keeping a dog on a leash out here in what is practically country is pretty tough on a dog," Uncle Al said. "Suppose I have Hank keep a closer eye on him. Then if he continues to bother you I guess we'll have to tie him up."

"I'm not interested in promises," Mr. Apple said.

Agony is a smart dog and I always will think he heard what was being said, and knew that he had to do something if he wanted to keep his liberty. He must have been hiding around the corner. Also, Siegfried gave him wonderful cooperation. There was a small squeak from the

93

Thursday, July 11th

Midge and I were right. We did strike oil. There wasn't quite as much there as we had expected, but we hit oil all right. Uncle Al was right too about saying it was not advisable to try and buy up all the land around here.

It was ten o'clock before we were set to try pumping our well. News certainly gets around in a tiny place like Grover's Corner. I don't know how everybody heard about our oil well, but a crowd appeared out of nowhere. I guess people weren't quite as doubting as they acted. Aunt Mabel came over, Midge's mother, almost every other housewife in Grover's Corner, the man who was driving the bulldozer where the new house is being built, the milkman, the man who picks up laundry, and even Mr. Marble shut down his drilling rig for a little while. I don't know whether someone called the newspaper or whether Mr. Sylvester just happened by. He is the man who took the pictures of the buggy and the bathtub. Anyhow, he was on hand when we connected up the pump. We put the hose down in the well and set the little hand pump on a box, and I began pumping. Midge held a big galvanized steel bucket.

At first the connection wasn't tight and the pump kept sucking air. Then Mr. Marble tightened it and I tried pumping again. I had made about ten or twelve strokes when oil spouted out and into the bucket. Instead of everybody cheering as I'd expected, they all looked sort of silly. Mr. Marble said, "Well, I'll be a horned toad!" I pumped the bucket about half full and then stopped. Mr. Sylvester stepped forward, stuck his finger in the bucket, and held it up to his nose. Then he rubbed his fingers together as Uncle Al had done the night before. "It's oil," he said. "You kids really have discovered oil!"

Everybody began to get excited at this point. There was a lot of noise and two or three of the women rushed back home to telephone their friends. I guess everybody in that area would have been drilling wells in their back yards inside of another fifteen minutes if it hadn't been for Midge's father.

Mr. Glass had worked until two o'clock at the laboratory, so he didn't go to work this morning but slept late. I guess he got up about ten and found that he was alone in the house. He went downstairs and had some toast and coffee, and then, noticing the crowd across the street, came over to investigate. Instead of sticking his finger in the oil as everyone else had done, he picked up a stick and stirred it a little and let it drip back into the bucket.

"Oil!" Midge said, gloating. "I'll be known as the oil queen of New Jersey."

"It's oil, all right," Mr. Glass admitted. "It's been ten years since I had much to do with oil and I never was an expert, but just off-hand I'd say this wasn't crude oil. It looks more like one of the lighter grades of bunker fuel oil."

Monday, July 29th

I have half a notion to write the postmaster general and tell him what I think of the way the mail is being handled at Grover's Corner. I suppose most rural mail carriers are pretty nice people, but the one who delivers the mail to us isn't very cooperative or very intelligent for that matter. Of course, from the things he said, I guess he doesn't think much of Midge or me either, so things are about balanced.

For the past two or three days we haven't had even one rabbit. Midge had the idea that if we let Mathilda out of the pen to run loose, she might decoy Jedidiah back with her.

"And she might get as wild as he is," I objected.

"Not if we don't leave her out too long," Midge said. "I've let her go several times and she lets me walk right up to her."

I finally agreed, because one rabbit alone isn't much good when you want to raise rabbits to sell. Anyhow, we let Mathilda out. Midge was right; at first she was able to walk up to the rabbit without much trouble. For a while it looked as if the scheme might work. That evening, about dusk, Mathilda came hopping up to the pen and Jedidiah was with her. We had left one end of the pen open and the plan was to wait until they were both inside eating, and then to slip up and close the opening. Jedidiah went inside and he seemed hungry. However, he wasn't so hungry that he forgot to keep an eye on us. Midge was within three feet of the pen when he bolted out and ran for the tree.

We left the pen open, and I suppose Mathilda hopped back out after she had eaten. We saw them several times yesterday but we didn't get very close. I don't know whether Mathilda had decided she liked freedom too or was just following Jedidiah, but she hopped away too. Midge began to get worried.

"He's a bad influence," she said. "I should never have let Mathilda go out with him."

This morning about ten-thirty, as I was walking toward the lot, I saw both rabbits beneath a rose bush in the Millers' front yard. I hurried to the barn to get a net and then over to get Midge for help. She got her father's fishing net and came along.

Both rabbits were facing the same way, and I don't know whether they were dozing or not, but we crept up quietly until we were only a few feet behind them. They didn't move. We have had a lot of practice trying to catch Jedidiah with a hand net, so I suppose we had to do it right sooner or later. We both pounced at once. Our timing was perfect and Midge got one rabbit and I got the other.

"Hurrah! I'm a member of the firm!" Midge shouted.

I had caught Mathilda and Midge had Jedidiah. I reached in and got Mathilda by the nape of the neck and pulled her out of the net, kicking and squirming like mad. A big rabbit like that is not easy to hold. Finally I got her cradled in my left arm, still holding onto the loose skin of her neck with my right hand. Then she quieted down.

Midge had a much rougher time. Jedidiah was wild, and he wasn't giving up without a fight. He kicked and ripped a hole in the net. Afraid that he would ruin the net, Midge lifted him out. He came out easily enough, but then he really began acting up. Her arms were bare and in a couple of seconds he had scratched her left arm so badly in several places that it was all over blood.

"I can't hold him much longer," she said. "What will I do?"

We were standing beside the Millers' mailbox. Grover's Corner is on a rural mail route, and everyone has sheet-metal mailboxes on posts out beside the road. The Millers' mailbox is a big one, and suddenly it occurred to me that we could use it.

"Stuff him in there," I suggested.

Midge yanked open the mailbox, shoved Jedidiah inside, and slammed the lid shut again. The lid fits tightly,

friend, and I went along. We didn't get back until after five. While Aunt Mabel was getting dinner Uncle Al and I walked down to the lot. Midge had said something about going to Trenton and I didn't know whether she had fed the rabbit or not.

As we approached the lot I heard voices, but I didn't think anything about it because there are people living on both sides and across the street. Then as we rounded the corner of the barn I heard a couple of bangs and I saw Mr. and Mrs. Apple. He was stomping on what remained of my box trap, which wasn't much.

"Hey, that's my trap!" I said.

Mr. Apple looked startled, but he didn't back down an inch. "I have just destroyed it," he said, shaking his head and drawing himself up as tall as he could, which isn't very tall.

Uncle Al looked at him as though he didn't believe what he'd heard. "And why, might I ask?"

"Because my poor cat has been a prisoner in it all day," said Mrs. Apple indignantly. "I've a good notion to report this to the SPCA. I don't know what this boy has against my cat, but it's quite obvious that he enjoys being mean to it."

"I didn't set that trap for your cat," I said. "I set it for Jedidiah, our white rabbit. It had a carrot in it. I don't know what your cat was doing, going in to get a carrot."

Uncle Al was beginning a slow burn. He drew a deep breath and said, "I might point out that the trap was not set on your property and that in order to be caught in it your cat had to be trespassing. I might also point out that you too are trespassing. This lad went to a lot of trouble to build that box trap, and your destroying it was entirely uncalled for. You claim that my nephew seems to have it in for your cat. I think it's the other way around. You seem to have it in for him."

"I have nothing against your nephew," said Mr. Apple, "or against this little girl here."

I turned around and there stood Midge. When she had appeared I don't know, but naturally she wasn't going to miss a good fight.

"These two children have created a public nuisance here on this lot," Mr. Apple continued. "From the minute that sign was painted on the end of the barn we have not had a moment's privacy. Half the day that dog is letting out unearthly sounds, and he seems to spend half his time chasing a white rabbit back and forth across my place, with these two children yelling encouragement. There is always some sort of chaos going on. The road has been blocked by strange contraptions and crowds have gathered because of some silly report about oil. People have parked in my driveway, tramped across my lawn, honked their horns in front of our door, and generally made our

161

life miserable. The other night we had to do without power for several hours and I understand that this young man was indirectly responsible. We moved to the country for some privacy, Mr. Harris, and until your nephew appeared we enjoyed it."

"I like peace and quiet myself," Uncle Al said slowly. "I appreciate your desire for privacy. However, I don't think my nephew has trespassed on your property, have you, Hank?"

"I haven't set foot on the place," I said, "and neither has Midge."

"It is quite possible that the dog has run across your property several times, just as your cat has killed our birds," Uncle Al said. "As for other people tramping across your lawn or parking in your driveway, I'm sorry, but that is not my nephew's fault or responsibility. He didn't invite them here. While you have a right to your privacy, he has a right to the normal pursuits of a boy his age. If he wants to yell and chase a white rabbit, then as far as I'm concerned he can. He's on his own property here and he can yell his head off for all of me. In the future, stay off this property and don't do anything like smashing that box trap again or I'll take you to court."

"I would be very happy to be taken to court on the subject of the box trap," Mr. Apple said. "In case you haven't read the game laws, you might be interested to know that trapping rabbits is illegal in this state. I intend to make a

Tuesday, August 6th

The firm of Henry Reed, Inc., went into the mushroom business today. I doubt if you'd call hunting mushrooms research. Probably just plain ordinary search would be better. Whether it was research or not, it was profitable. Midge and I made about four dollars in about two hours and a half.

Aunt Mabel says it was the damp weather after a dry spell that caused the mushrooms to come out the way they did. She claims she's never seen them so plentiful before. They were growing all over our side lawn and out in the pasture behind Midge's house. We got a great big basket and filled it in no time this morning. Aunt Mabel went over all of them carefully to make certain that there were no poisonous mushrooms and then we divided them up into smaller baskets. She bought two baskets at fifty cents each, Midge's mother bought two, and altogether we sold eight right here at Grover's Corner. There were still plenty out in the pasture, but we had exhausted the market.

Agony was feeling fine today and doesn't seem to have suffered any damage from his afternoon in the culvert.

He went mushroom-hunting with us. Each time we picked one, he'd sniff at the ground where it had been broken off and start digging. He seemed to like the smell of them, so tonight when Aunt Mabel had some for dinner I gave Agony several in his dish. He ate them immediately and seemed to enjoy them.

After dinner I came upstairs and found a book on mushrooms in my mother's nature library. She had a twenty-volume encyclopedia on nature and about forty other books. I'd like to take them all back to Naples with me but it costs a lot to ship books back and forth across the ocean. That is probably why she didn't take them with her in the first place.

I read about how to tell edible mushrooms from poisonous ones and looked at all the pictures. It seems there isn't any foolproof way of testing mushrooms to make certain which are safe to eat. You simply have to know them. There are certainly more different kinds of mushrooms than I had any idea there were. I was thumbing through the book looking at the pictures when I came to a section on truffles. There was a picture of a man in France using a pig to find truffles. I once saw a man hunt truffles with a truffle hound in Italy, so naturally I read the article. It was very interesting and it gave me a wonderful idea. The author said that a few truffles had been found in America but that none of the really delicious ones had been discovered yet. He saw no reason why they shouldn't be found in America, though, and believes that the man who finds them will probably be famous and will make a great deal of money. That decided me. Agony is not only a smart dog but he has an unusually keen nose. Since he likes mushrooms anyhow, he should make an excellent truffle hound.

Everything is working out fine. The firm of Henry Reed, Inc., is going to do space research. We've got all the material and I've figured out how to do it.

There was a lot of noise in the field out back of Uncle Al's house early this morning, so after breakfast I went out to investigate. Mr. Baines, who farms the land, was cutting the grass with a machine he calls a forage harvester. This cuts the grass and clover, chops it in pieces, and blows it into a big wagon. When he had filled the wagon Midge and I rode on it to the farm. There were two station wagons there and four or five men. They were from the Agricultural Experiment Station at Rutgers and they were working with Mr. Baines on a new method of making silage. They took the chopped-up grass and dumped it in great big plastic bags which they then sealed. They said it would keep inside these bags all winter if necessary.

The plastic bags were about ten feet long and at least four feet in diameter. They seemed quite tough. I asked them for one and they said if there were any left over I could have one, so I went back about five-thirty. They were gone but they had left a bag behind for me as they had promised.

A plastic bag like that will make a perfect balloon. I remembered reading an article earlier in the summer about a man who went up a long way in a balloon. I found the magazine and read the article again. Sure enough, his balloon was made of plastic, so my silage bag is going to be just what I need.

Tuesday, August 20th

I went to the library today and read everything that I could find on balloons. It seems the Army and Navy and Air Force and the weather service all use a lot of balloons. One of their troubles is that if they send a balloon up with instruments, such as thermometers and barometers, half the time they never get the balloon or the instruments back. Sometimes they send up bigger balloons with all sorts of complicated radio equipment which automatically sends back information. These are very expensive and if there's much of a wind they often lose these too. Then of course there are the biggest balloons, which go up with a gondola that will carry a man. Naturally they always take a lot of precautions with these because the men who go up want to come back in one piece. They object to being lost with the balloon.

I've thought quite a bit about it and I've decided that I could do everybody a great service if I could develop a medium-size balloon, say about the size of my big plastic silage bag, that would be very cheap but would carry some instruments which would always get back. I have what I think is a brilliant idea. I can send up homing pigeons in the balloon and they can fly back. Of course a pigeon wouldn't be able to carry a very heavy instrument, so any thermometers or barometers that were sent up with the balloon would have to be small enough to be strapped to the pigeon's leg, but if I can work out all the other details the armed forces ought to be able to figure out how to make small instruments.

A real trained homing pigeon would be best, naturally, but all pigeons tend to find their way back home. I don't intend to waste time finding just the right pigeon because I haven't got much time. I have to fly back to Naples next week. Uncle Al got the ticket today. There'll be just time enough for me to finish my experiments in space research with my plastic balloon. If my idea works, Henry Reed, Inc., should really be on the map. I expect I'll be made a lieutenant in the Army and Navy and at least a general in the Air Force.

I asked Uncle Al about the pigeons again at dinner tonight. He says they are all part homing or racing pigeons and probably would be able to find their way home from quite a distance. Anyhow, I'm sure they'll do and I'm going to slip over as soon as it gets dark and catch a good healthy one.

Wednesday, August 21st

I told Midge about my idea today and she thinks it sounds wonderful. She was a little doubtful at first that we would be able to work out all the details but before the day was over we had practically everything figured out. In fact, I think we should be able to send up our balloon tomorrow.

We did some of the preliminary work today. We took the pigeon that I caught last night and went down the

road half a mile with it, carrying it in a basket. Then we
let it out. It flew straight back home. I'd put a red leg band
around it so there wasn't any mistake. There it was sitting
on top of the barn. If I can, I'll catch the same pigeon
again tonight.

We found a round wicker basket in Midge's basement
which Mrs. Glass gave to us. This afternoon I built a small
slotted cage for the pigeon. It has a little door that slides
up and down. The problem of how to release the pigeon
after he has been up in the air for a while was a tough one.
And for a while I didn't think we could solve it. Midge
gave me the idea.

"We'll have to put the pigeon to sleep somehow," she
said. "Then we can send an alarm clock up in the basket
with him to wake him up after he's been up for say half
an hour."

Of course she was just kidding but it gave me an idea. Aunt Mabel has an old-fashioned round alarm clock upstairs in the guest room. She didn't want to part with it at first but I offered to buy it and finally she gave it to me. When the alarm goes off, the little thumb screw or handle on the back that you use to wind the alarm goes around and around. I fastened a wire to this and a string to the wire. When the alarm goes off it winds up the string. The string runs over a pulley and is attached to the little door of my pigeon cage and it gradually raises the door. It looks sort of complicated and homemade but it works. Midge and I tried it three or four times and it opened the door every time. We are all set and tomorrow is the great day.

Thursday, August 22nd

We had the great balloon ascension today. The balloon went up and it came down. I don't know whether you would call it a success or not because it didn't work out exactly as Midge and I had planned. I don't think we will be as famous as I had hoped, but it isn't really our fault. Still I'm going to write the Air Force and tell them my scheme. Maybe they can try it out in the middle of a desert someplace where they won't be bothered by all the complications that we ran into. I guess the best way to explain just why the experiment wasn't completely successful is to tell everything that happened today.

It took us much longer to get the balloon ready than we had expected. There was considerable work and also we had some interruptions. We spent a good part of the morning chasing Mr. Baines's sheep. Mr. Baines had turned about thirty sheep into the pasture out back of my lot. They found a hole in the fence someplace. At least, eight of them did. We were busy working on the balloon, trying to attach the basket to the plastic bag, when suddenly these sheep walked through the woods and stood there staring at us. We thought we would chase them back where they came from but when I went to look I couldn't find the hole. Maybe they jumped the fence, I don't know.

They weren't bothering us so we let them graze a while on the lot, but then they wandered out toward the road. Three of them started across just as a big green sedan came by. Grover's Corner is such a little place it isn't really a town at all, and a lot of people don't even slow down when they go through. This man must have been going sixty miles an hour and he missed those sheep by inches. He swerved and there was a screech of tires and his car rocked back and forth. He managed to get it under control again but it was certainly close.

We went across the street to Midge's house and tried to call Mr. Baines but no one answered the phone. I don't know whether he was away or out in the fields.

We went back to the lot to see what had happened to the sheep but when we arrived they had disappeared. We thought they had gone back where they came from but a few minutes later we heard a "baa."

"They're over at Apple's," said Midge. "I bet he loves that." The thought of it tickled her so much that she sat down and laughed about it.

I wanted to see exactly what he would do when he discovered the sheep and we took time out to go over by the hedge. The sheep weren't in the front yard so we went on back to where we could look into the back part of his lot. There were the sheep, all eight of them, inside the wire enclosure or pen that Mr. Apple had built. The gate had evidently been left open and they had simply walked in.

"I wonder why he hasn't noticed them," I said. "Usually he's out here with a cannon if a sparrow lands on the place."

"I know," said Midge. "They aren't home. I saw them driving out in their car right after breakfast this morning. She was all dressed up so I suppose they went to New York or Philadelphia or someplace to go shopping."

"If those sheep do wander into the front yard they'll eat all her flowers," I said. "Maybe I ought to slip over and close that gate. They can't do any harm in there."

"That's not a bad idea," said Midge, "but I think we ought to do it for Mr. Baines rather than for Mr. Apple. It will keep his sheep from getting killed on the highway."

I slipped through a hole in the hedge, walked across the lawn, and closed the gate to the wire pen. The sheep were busily eating and didn't bother to look up.

About eleven o'clock Midge went over to her house for something and she called Mr. Baines again. This time Mrs. Baines answered. Mr. Baines had gone with his hired man to some auction sale where he hoped to buy some dairy cows, and would not be back until later. She said he would be over in his truck to get the sheep as soon as he got home. That was settled, so we forgot about the sheep and went back to our balloon.

There's no use going into all the details with the troubles

we had getting the basket attached and getting my pigeon cage rigged up just right. We spent most of the morning at it and so it was after lunch before we went to get the cylinder of gas. This was too heavy to handle and I had to go back and get Uncle Al's tractor and cart.

We had quite a time getting the balloon inflated. I had read enough to know that you don't inflate a balloon all the way so that it's nice and fat like a sausage. Instead it should be only half full and look sort of limp. Then as it goes higher and higher the gas expands and the balloon fills out.

It took us half an hour to locate a hose to attach to the cylinder to use for inflating the plastic bag. Finally we managed it. About three-thirty we had the balloon inflated just right and it was tugging at the ropes. Everything looked promising.

I'd caught the same pigeon the night before and I got him and put him in the little slotted cage. I hooked up the alarm clock and set the alarm to go off in about fifteen minutes. I didn't have any instruments to strap to the pigeon's leg, but since this was just an experimental run we figured that wasn't necessary. The main idea was to prove that it would work. From the way the balloon kept tugging at that anchor rope there wasn't much doubt that it would work.

"What if it goes up too fast?" Midge asked.

"How can it go up too fast?" I said.

"Well, then, too far," she said. "Supposing it goes up so far that the pigeon can't breathe. Doesn't the air get thinner the higher you go?"

I had to admit that it did but I doubted if our balloon would get up that high. However, Midge kept worrying about it.

"Well, I'll tell you what we'll do," I said. "We'll put a couple of bricks in the gondola to add a little weight. We can let it go up a way on a rope to get an idea how far and how fast it will go up."

The trouble was that we didn't have a long rope. The balloon was tied with a piece of clothesline and that was only a few feet long. "A really good strong twine would do the trick," I said. "Do you suppose you could find a ball?"

"I think so," Midge said and started to go across the street to her house. She had gone only a few feet when she turned around and said, "What about witnesses?"

"What do you mean, witnesses?"

"We ought to have someone who sees all this and can swear to it afterwards. Even the Wright brothers had a few people watching."

I had to admit that she had a good point. The only trouble was that if we invited a lot of people over to see our great experiment and then it flopped, we would feel foolish, just as we had when they discovered that our oil well wasn't an oil well at all. I certainly thought it would work, but so did all those Air Force scientists when they fired their first rockets down in Florida. Instead they blew up. I didn't know what to do.

"I know," said Midge. "We can take pictures."

That was a wonderful idea, and we both decided to get our cameras.

It was about twenty minutes to four when I walked into the kitchen. Aunt Mabel had just taken some cookies out of the oven but I was so excited that I didn't wait to get one of them. I rushed upstairs, got my camera, and hurried back toward the lot. Midge was crossing the street as I approached and we reached the barn together. Agony as usual was tagging along with me.

We had tied the balloon out in the middle of the lot where it would be clear of the trees when it started up. There was a big stump there and I had driven a spike into this. There was a loop in our anchor rope and this had been slipped over the end of the spike. The wicker basket was about six inches off the ground, suspended by four ropes from the bottom of the plastic bag.

We stopped and took pictures of our balloon from several angles and then I found several bricks. Since I had put the pigeon in his cage, all we had to do was put the bricks in the basket and let it make an experimental flight tied to Midge's string. We walked up to it, neither of us suspecting a thing, and so we were both flabbergasted when we looked inside. There sitting in the basket was

Siegfried, the Apples' white cat. He had knocked over the alarm clock, upset the cage, managed to get the door open somehow, and had killed the pigeon. When he saw us he glared at us and started waving his tail back and forth as though daring us to take the pigeon away from him.

I've never seen anybody as mad as Midge was. She was so mad she couldn't say a word, which means that she was as mad as she can possibly get. She sputtered and stuttered and jumped up and down. I looked around for a stick. In the first place Siegfried is a big cat and I didn't want to tangle with him with my bare hands. And secondly I wanted the stick to give him a couple of good swats, but before I could find one Midge thought of something else.

"I hope you go up so high you never come back," she said, and she reached out and grabbed the rope. Just at that moment Agony either smelled the cat, or saw him, or heard him, or found out somehow what was going on. He came rushing up from behind me and made a leap. He landed in the wicker basket just as Midge pulled the anchor rope off the spike. Midge said later that she was in such a rage she didn't realize for a minute that Agony had jumped into the basket. By the time she did it was too late.

With both the cat and the dog, and of course the dead pigeon, in the basket, the balloon didn't go up very fast. There is really no excuse for my not having caught the anchor rope. I guess I didn't understand what Midge had done for a minute. By this time the balloon was quite a way up in the air. I rushed over and made a leap for the end of the rope but just missed it.

"Agony's in there!" I said to Midge.

Midge nodded dumbly. "Yes I know he is," she said.

We both stood there like a couple of idiots while the balloon kept getting higher and higher. We were sort of hypnotized and we stood watching as it kept moving on toward the tops of the trees.

I doubt if either Agony or Siegfried knew what was happening for the first minute or two. As the balloon drifted upward, for a while I could hear Siegfried spitting. Then he let out an angry yowl and a minute later there was a yip from Agony. I suppose Siegfried scratched him. Then Siegfried's head appeared above the edge of the basket. I think he was about to jump out but suddenly he saw he was up in the air and couldn't, and after that I guess he was just too terrified to fight Agony any more.

"What are we going to do?" Midge asked in a scared voice.

"I don't know," I admitted.

The balloon reached the level of the treetops and began drifting slowly over toward Apple's. Midge and I traipsed along after it. I don't know what we planned to do but I felt I had to trail that balloon and get Agony down somehow.

The balloon just missed the big oak tree and then went over above Mr. Apple's lawn. Midge and I followed as far as the hedge and stood looking through it. There was scarcely any breeze and the balloon moved very slowly. If Agony hadn't been in the basket it would have been a beautiful sight and I would have been proud of it. As it was I was just plain scared.

It drifted on with the basket swinging back and forth gently beneath the big plastic bag. Then it passed directly over the Apples' house. As it did Siegfried poked his head over the edge of the wicker basket and saw his chance. I'll have to admit that he is a pretty smart cat. He didn't hesitate but jumped. The basket was about eight feet above the roof but of course that was no jump at all for Siegfried. The roof is a steep, gabled slate affair and certainly not a very good place for a landing field. Only a cat could have done it without slipping down and over the edge. As it was, Siegfried very nearly lost his hold. He

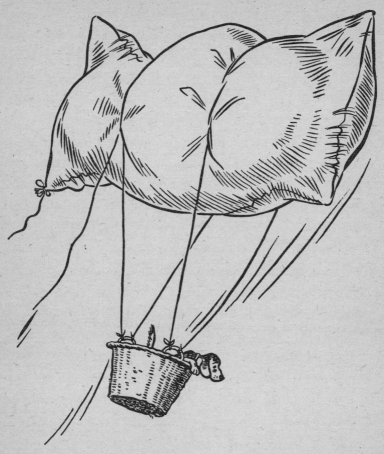

managed to get one paw over the peak as he landed. Somehow he pulled himself up and crouched there. He was
too scared to stir.

I suppose Agony wondered what had become of the
cat and he poked his head over the edge. It was the first
time I'd seen him since he'd jumped in the basket and I

imagine it was the first time he realized that he was up in the air. I would like to have seen the expression on his face. At the time, however, all I was worried about was that he might become panicky and jump.

"Stay in there, Agony," I shouted. "We'll get you down."

I didn't know how I was going to get him down but I was hoping. Up until this time Midge and I had followed along like a couple of big oafs, fascinated by that sight of that balloon up in the air, and not really thinking at all. Slowly we began to come out of it.

"Well, I might as well take some pictures," Midge said. "I guess Agony's on his way out into the great blue yonder. Maybe I can win a prize with my picture."

"I'm going to go see if somebody can't help us," I said.

For the first time I halfway wished that Agony's original owner would appear and want his dog. I would have been glad to see anyone who would help me get Agony back down to earth again. But no one did appear and I started running for home. At least I could ask Aunt Mabel for advice.

About halfway home I saw Mr. Ainsworth standing in his yard, looking up in the sky with a puzzled expression on his face.

"Is that contraption something of yours?" he asked.

I nodded. "It's a balloon, but my dog got in the basket by mistake and I've got to get him down!"

"Your beagle's in there?" Mr. Ainsworth asked.

Again I nodded. "Who do you think I should call? The state police? Do you suppose they could help me?"

"Maybe you'd better call out the Army and they could shoot it down." Then suddenly he grinned. "That's it," he said. "That isn't up so high. Maybe I can shoot it down for you. Come on."

We hurried to his house where he got out a .22 rifle. Then we got in his car and drove down the road. Midge was back by the road by this time and we picked her up too.

The balloon had drifted on and was over the middle of a big pasture beyond the Apples'. We got out of the car and hurried into the pasture a short distance. Mr. Ainsworth looked around carefully and then up at the balloon. "A twenty-two long will carry about a mile," he said. "I want to be sure where the bullet is going to land before I go firing up in the air."

I wasn't too keen on the idea of his firing that .22 in Agony's direction. "Are you sure you can hit the balloon without hitting the basket?" I asked.

Mr. Ainsworth looked at me and snorted. "Son, I've hunted ducks for forty-five years. I may be sixty-seven years old but my hand's still pretty steady. If I can't hit that balloon without killing your dog, then I'll take up knitting."

He raised his gun and fired. He waited a second and fired twice more.

225

"The trouble with this set-up is you can't tell whether you hit it or not. I think I've hit that bag but I'll give it a couple of more shots and then we'll wait and see what happens."

The balloon was still rising slowly and was probably another twenty-five or thirty feet higher than when it had passed over Mr. Apple's house. It was also drifting very gradually across the field. We followed a short distance behind. Mr. Ainsworth fired three times more before we reached the fence.

"That's got at least four or five holes in it," he said. "The trouble is that there isn't much pressure inside the bag to force the gas out."

"If the holes are up near the top, the gas will leak out," I said. "Of course it may take quite a while through little holes like that."

"All right, we'll make sure there's some near the top," he said, and he fired another three shots.

We all stood at the fence for several minutes, watching the balloon closely. When it had drifted almost to the far side of the next field, I climbed over the fence to go after it.

"I think it's settling a little," said Mr. Ainsworth. "It's certainly not rising any more. You go on ahead and follow it. I'll go get in the car and drive around and down Maple Road. That's straight ahead about three fields over. By the time it reaches that we should be able to tell what it's doing."

226

Mr. Ainsworth was right. It was fifteen minutes later before we were positive the balloon was settling, and I had to follow it about half a mile beyond Maple Road, but it did settle. Toward the last it came down rather fast and for a few minutes I was scared it would come down too fast and that Agony would be hurt. The basket landed with a bump but Agony jumped out uninjured. He was really glad to see me.

Mr. Ainsworth came up and together we examined the plastic bag. It was full of holes. I think almost every shot he fired must have hit.

"I'm certainly glad I found you," I said. "You saved Agony's life."

"I enjoyed doing it," said Mr. Ainsworth. "It isn't every day that a man gets to shoot down a balloon carrying a beagle."

Mr. Ainsworth dropped us off at the barn. There wasn't much left of all our equipment. The balloon was full of holes, the pigeon was dead, the alarm clock didn't seem to work any more, and the wicker basket hadn't been much good to begin with. Both Midge and I felt pretty discouraged.

"Some day I'll kill that cat," Midge said.

"Hey, what about the cat?" I asked. "Do you suppose he's still up there on the roof?"

We hurried over to the hedge and looked through. Siegfried was still clinging to the peak of the roof. He knew better than to move because those slates were slippery.

"How do you suppose the Apples are going to get him down from there?"

"I think they should get him down the same way we got Agony down," Midge said. "Shoot him down."

"The Apples still aren't home," I said, looking at their empty garage.

"They'll have a nice pleasant surprise when they do get back," Midge said and started laughing. "I'll bet that will keep Mr. Apple busy for a while—figuring out how that cat got up there."

It was a funny idea and we both sat down and laughed about it for a while. There just wasn't any possible way that cat could have gotten up there except by being dropped from an airplane or balloon.

"Don't worry," said Midge. "They'll blame us anyhow. Mrs. Apple will claim that you picked up the cat by the tail and threw him up there."

"I wonder how soon they'll be back," I said. "Sooner or later that cat will either try to make a move or he'll get so tired he can't hang on any longer. If he falls he'll be killed."

"Well, I'm not going to go over and hold a net and wait for him," Midge said. "I don't feel a bit sorry for him."

She did though, and we both got more and more worried. There was a big tree toward the front of the house and I had the idea that if the cat could be coaxed up in that direction he might be able to make a leap into the tree. Midge and I walked out to the road to take a look. When we got there we saw that it would be a pretty long leap.

"They might stay out to dinner for all we know," I said. "They've been gone since early this morning."

"All right," Midge said finally. "I suppose we'd better call the Fire Department. I'll do it but I'm not going to say who I am, because whatever happens the Apples are going to be sore."

The hook-and-ladder truck arrived at about quarter to five, just when people began returning from work. Everyone thought there was a fire and stopped. People are naturally curious and I guess they would as soon see a cat rescued as watch a fire. Anyhow, inside of fifteen minutes there must have been thirty cars parked beside the road and there was a whole group gathered on Mr. Apple's lawn. Among them was Mr. Glass and my Uncle Al, but Midge and I stayed very carefully on our side of the hedge. We didn't see how anyone could connect us with that cat being on the roof, and we wanted to keep it that way.

The firemen got the ladder up and a man was halfway up to the edge of the roof when the Apples came home. Mr. Apple was too scared to be nasty at first. I suppose he thought his house was on fire. They got out of the car and one of the firemen told Mrs. Apple the cause of all the excitement. She looked up, and when she saw Siegfried on the peak of the roof she very nearly fainted. Mr. Apple and a fireman helped her over to a garden bench where she sat down.

"How do you suppose that cat got up there?" one of the firemen asked.

Mr. Apple just shook his head. We could hear everyone talking from where we stood at the hedge and they all seemed to be puzzled.

After the fireman reached the edge of the roof he still had to put up another short ladder and hook it over the peak in order to get to Siegfried. He finally did it, though, and Siegfried was so glad to get down that he didn't scratch the fireman.

Everything had gone very well up to this point. The Apples were acting almost human. Mrs. Apple was full of thanks to the firemen and Mr. Apple hadn't screamed at anybody for being on his lawn. A tall, sandy-haired man who had appeared with the Apples stood over by a lilac bush watching everything and saying nothing. Just when it appeared that all the excitement was over there were a couple of loud baas from the big back yard beyond the hedge. Midge and I looked at each other in surprise. Mr. Baines still hadn't come for his sheep.

Mr. Apple was surprised too, and then he was suspicious. He hurried over to the hedge and looked through the opening. From the bellow he gave you would have thought he was being murdered. He jumped up and down and shouted something that I couldn't understand, and he looked as though he were going to have apoplexy. I guess everybody else thought the same thing and they all hurried over to find out what was the matter. Of course none of them understood why he was so mad and after they had looked through the hedge they still didn't know anything more than they had before. Midge and I hurried back to see what he would do. We arrived just in time to see him open the gate and rush inside his wire fence. He screamed and shouted and waved his arms. Of course the poor sheep were scared half out of their wits. They all rushed through the gate and went running out through the gap in the hedge into the front yard.

There wasn't much left of the grass inside the fence. After all, eight sheep had been there all day and they had had nothing to do but eat. It was cropped down almost to the roots. They had made a very thorough and very clean job of it. It wouldn't need mowing for a long time. Apple pointed at the ground, dancing up and down, and I wasn't certain whether he was going to cry or blow up. The sandy-haired man walked over, went through the gate, and stood talking with Apple for several minutes. Mr. Apple calmed down a little bit but he was still quite excited. The sheep went baaing off down the road but, as I said to Midge, I thought we had done our duty by them. It wasn't our fault if Mr. Apple let them out on the road to be killed.

Some of the people stood around a few minutes longer,

wondering what in the world had happened to Mr. Apple. However, there wasn't anything else to see. The fire truck drove away and soon everyone had gone home. It was dinner time so Midge and I went home too.

Aunt Mabel was home when I got there but she had been up to the road a few minutes earlier, watching Siegfried's rescue. Uncle Al didn't appear for another ten minutes.

"Well, that was quite a lot of excitement," Aunt Mabel said as we sat down to dinner. "How on earth do you suppose that cat got up there?"

"No one seems to know," Uncle Al said, looking at me. "However I was talking to Mr. Ainsworth just before I came in."

I could tell from Uncle Al's expression that he suspected something. After all it wasn't my fault that Siegfried had jumped in the basket and there was no reason why I shouldn't tell them what had happened, so I did. All the time that I was explaining things Uncle Al kept running his hand over his face.

"If I hadn't grown up with your mother I would swear all this was a dream," he said when I finished.

"What on earth was Mr. Apple screaming about there at the last?" Aunt Mabel asked.

"Oh, that," Uncle Al said. "That is the explanation of our little mystery about all his objections to trespassing. That tall fellow in the brown suit was Jim Weber. He used to be

232

county agent around here years ago, and now he's with a seed company in Philadelphia. I thought I recognized him and later on I went over and talked to him. That's why I was a little late getting back. It seems that Mr. Apple has developed some new kind of grass. Or at least he thinks he has. Now, this may sound ridiculous, but his grass is supposed to grow in a sort of a spiral. It's a curly grass and doesn't need mowing very often. He's got some idea that it's immensely valuable and it may be, although Weber says that such discoveries or developments never make a great deal of money. Anyhow, Apple has been working on four or five strains of grass and this is the one he considers to be the final answer. He thinks it will make him famous. He planted a plot in the back yard behind that hedge and put up a wire enclosure around it. According to Weber he's been so secretive and mysterious about it that it's ridiculous. I guess he was afraid someone would steal his secret. Anyhow, after a lot of negotiations and fiddle-faddle, he arranged for a seed company to send a representative up to see this great discovery. Jim Weber was the man they sent. The trouble is that when he did get out to look at it they found that some sheep had been locked up inside the enclosure and had eaten practically all the grass."

Uncle Al paused and looked at me. "How did those sheep get in there?" he asked.

I guess Uncle Al must be what they call psychic because there wasn't any possible way that he could know that I

233

had anything to do with those sheep being in Mr. Apple's enclosure. "They got through a hole in the fence at the back of our lot," I explained. "Midge and I chased them and they went through the hedge into Mr. Apple's place. Of course that *would* be the only time that he ever left the gate open to his grass plot. I guess that grass must be good. The sheep went right in there and started eating it. I slipped over and closed the gate and Midge called Mr. Baines. We forgot all about them until we heard Mr. Apple scream. Besides we didn't know that was special grass."

"Well, Mr. Apple is very disappointed," said Uncle Al, "and I can't say that I blame him, but after all if he hadn't been so mysterious you'd have known that he was anxious to protect that grass and would have chased the sheep out instead of locking them in. Anyhow, Jim Weber told him this would be a good test of the grass. If it comes back it will be proof that it's tough."

Monday, August 26th

My vacation is just about over. As Aunt Mabel said it's been a quiet summer. There've been no boys around to play baseball with, and things like that, but all in all things have been fairly interesting. I've enjoyed running a business and I've had a good time with Midge, even though she is a girl with a peculiar sense of humor.

I have my tickets and Uncle Al and Aunt Mabel are going to drive me over to the International Airport tomorrow morning. Midge is coming along. I hate to leave but on the other hand I'll be glad to see my father and mother.

I went down to the barn this morning to sort of close up shop, since I won't be around to run Henry Reed, Inc., at least for a while. I'm hoping to come back next summer though, and maybe my father will get a tour of duty in the United States. That would be nice.

We drew our money out of the bank last Friday and divided it. We had almost forty dollars each, which proves that free enterprise is profitable. I went down to the barn this morning to dump all the earthworms and dirt out of the tub. The pigeons can go on living there just as they did before, and Midge can take her rabbit back.

It was about nine-thirty when I got to the barn, and Midge had a ladder up against the end and was painting out my name with red barn paint.

"What are you doing?" I asked. I didn't like that at all. Here I hadn't even left and she was painting me right out of existence. I thought she was going to put up her name. After all it is still my property, or at least my mother's property.

"I'm getting it all set so that you can paint the new name," Midge explained. "Reed and Glass Enterprises, Inc. We've got to hurry because Mr. Sylvester will be back about noon to take a picture of it for his newspaper."

"How come?" I asked.

"Well, he came by a few minutes ago to ask about our balloon experiment. I don't know who told him about it but someone did. I told him the firm name was changed and he promised to take a picture and publish it in his paper. After all, it's only fair for my name to be up there because I'll be the only one around to represent the firm, at least until next summer."

Agony had been sniffing around in the grass, and he suddenly let out a bay and started across the lot. By this time I not only know his rabbit voice but the special rabbit voice that he uses when he chases the white rabbit. I looked up and there was the white rabbit streaking across the lot toward the woods.

"You still haven't kept your part of the bargain," I said.

236

"You were to contribute a pair of white rabbits and one of the pair is still loose."

"The agreement was two white rabbits," Midge said, "Nothing was said about exactly what two rabbits or what size. I've kept my part of the bargain. In fact, I've more than kept it. Really, my name ought to be first, but I won't argue about that."

"What are you talking about?" I asked suspiciously.

"Go over and look in the nest box," Midge said.

I did, and there were eight baby rabbits. They were just beginning to crawl out of the nest. Midge hadn't kept her part of the bargain the way either of us expected, but she certainly had contributed more than two rabbits.

"All right," I said. "Where's the white paint for the sign?"

"It and the small brush are just inside the door on the table," Midge said.

I had to wait until about noon for the barn paint to dry and then I painted the new name, REED AND GLASS ENTER-PRISES, INC. I was sort of glad to see it go up. Then I painted a smaller sign on a piece of cardboard saying "Rabbits for Sale, 75¢" and Midge put this on a stick right beside the road.

Tuesday, August 27th

I'm writing this on the plane flying over the ocean. Uncle Al, Aunt Mabel, Midge, and Agony all came to see me off. Uncle Al and Aunt Mabel are going to keep Agony for me. I doubt if anyone will claim him now, so he's mine for keeps. Maybe I can get him sent to Naples but there are a lot of customs restrictions and health requirements and things like that, so he may have to stay until I get back, which I hope will be next summer. Midge gave me a going-away present—an enlarged picture of the balloon as it went over Mr. Apple's house. Siegfried, the cat, was clinging to the roof and Agony was peeping over the edge of the basket. It was a very clear photograph and it proves that our invention will work.

Uncle Al said something peculiar just before I left. "Do me a favor, will you?" he asked. "When Vesuvius erupts, take a picture for me."

"Why?" I asked. "Do the volcanologists think it's going to erupt?" The reason I happen to know such a big word is that a very close friend of ours in Naples is a volcanologist. That's a man who spends all his time studying volcanoes.

238

Either Uncle Al knew the word or he figured out right away what it meant. "No, I haven't read of any predictions about its erupting," he said, "but *I* predict it will. With both you and your mother in Naples it's bound to."

I don't know what he was talking about and I don't think he does either, but, as I said before, sometimes I think he's psychic. I'm going to keep an eye on Vesuvius.

MS READ-a-thon—
a simple way to start
youngsters reading

Boys and girls between 6 and 14 can join the MS READ-a-thon and help find a cure for Multiple Sclerosis by reading books. And they get two rewards — the enjoyment of reading, and the great feeling that comes from helping others.

Parents and educators: For complete information call your local MS chapter. Or mail the coupon below.

Kids can help, too!

Mail to:
National Multiple Sclerosis Society
205 East 42nd Street
New York, N.Y. 10017
I would like more information about the MS READ-a-thon and how it can work in my area.

MS Mystery Sleuth

Name _____
(please print)
Address _____
City _____ State _____ Zip _____
Organization _____

1—80